For my mother, who is partial to a nice bit of cod - Simon

A TEMPLAR BOOK

First published in the UK in hardback in 2004 by Templar Publishing
This softback edition first published in 2005 by Templar Publishing,
an imprint of The Templar Company plc,
Pippbrook Mill, London Road, Dorking, Surrey, RH4 1JE, UK
www.templarco.co.uk

The illustrations for this book were painted in acrylics on paper.

First softback edition
Second impression

ISBN 1-84011-509-2

Designed by Mike Jolley
Edited by A. J. Wood

Printed in Belgium

For Archie
Best Wishes,
Simon Bartram

Dougal's
Deep-Sea
Diary

Simon Bartram

templar publishing

FRIDAY

7.30am   I woke with excitement.
I can't wait till tomorrow.

8.30   Train to work (no one talked to me as usual).
I wish tomorrow was here right NOW.

12.30pm   Lunch – too excited to eat (almost!).

3.30   Two hours to go.

4.30   One hour to go. Come on, clock!

5.29   Almost...

5.30   **HOLIDAY TIME! HURRAY!**

6.30   Home on train (no one talked to me as usual).

9.00   I packed my bags and went to bed early.
Tomorrow I, little old Dougal, will become...

SATURDAY

8.00am   I set off on the long coach trip to the harbour.
On the way I read about a city under the sea called
Atlantis – **WOW! Imagine that!**
Full of mermaids and stuff. I wish I could go there.
I love deep-sea diving, but I don't usually see
anything much. Maybe this time.

Arrived at the harbour very late.
Can't wait for the morning.

SUNDAY

7.43am   I found my boat for the week. It's very old and
rickety. I hope it doesn't sink.

9.32   Set sail.

9.33   Not sinking yet.

12.01pm   Mid-Atlantic. **1-2-3 SPLASH!**

My first dive of the week. It was beautiful.
So many fishy friends swam up to see me.
Last year I counted up to 121 different
types. I'm sure there are more this year.

I swam all day until my skin
went wrinkly.

MONDAY

10.00am I was asked to help with the Pacific dolphin show. All the dolphins performed well - apart from Herbert who just **couldn't** get it right.

6.00pm I had dinner in the diving capsule. The sharks looked at me hungrily. I think they wanted my salad.

NOT TODAY, BOYS!

9.14 BEDTIME — I dreamt of Atlantis and it seemed so **real.**

TUESDAY

10.43am Deep-sea dive time. I put on a very heavy suit and went deep, deep down. It was very dark and **I kept bumping into things**.

Didn't see anything interesting.
A most uneventful dive.

6.30pm I decided to have a quick evening dip, but I couldn't swim for long – the water was a little **nippy**!

9.30 I had a nice crab supper and went straight to bed...

...TUESDAY NIGHT

11.04   I was just about to fall asleep when it began to
rain. Pitter-patter, pitter-patter all night long.
Kept me awake for ages...

WEDNESDAY

6.58am   I eventually drifted off...

7.00   **RRRIIIIIIIIIINNNNNGGG!!!**
off went my alarm clock. I rubbed my eyes
and got out of bed. I felt tired and a little glum.

10.42am **WOW!**

On my first dive today I found an ancient treasure chest hidden in an old shipwreck. Inside were mostly coins (too old to use), two crowns (his and hers) and some hand-drawn maps of mysterious underwater worlds (wouldn't mind a closer peek at them!).

What a **fantastic morning!**

12.37pm Had forty winks.

2.15   I returned to the harbour. My good old friends, the dolphins, heaved the treasure to the surface. Herbert was the strongest, but for little Ralph it was all a bit of a strain.

3.15   The treasure was **big news**. The harbour was buzzing with activity. All the TV reporters wanted to interview me so I put on my favourite t-shirt and combed my beard.

9.03   I realised I'd forgotten to hand in the maps. I was a **little** worried.

9.04   Slept like a log.

THURSDAY

8.13am I was woken by sounds of excitement in the harbour. I looked out of the porthole and...

WHAT A SURPRISE!

The King and Queen were there and a beautiful new submarine glistened in the sea.

"In return," said the King, "for recovering the long lost treasure of our land, I now present you with this beautiful reward. May you sail the seas and dive forever and a day."

It was the finest thing I had ever seen, but I couldn't carry on diving forever, could I? Monday would soon come and my holiday would be over.

I would dive non-stop till then.

9.30am The crowds cheered as I climbed into the sub and disappeared deeper into the sea than I'd ever been before.

11.02 I remembered the old maps and had a quick peek. I was sure no one would mind. I followed their directions all day and all night until...

FRIDAY

8.29pm **WOW!**
There it was. I couldn't believe my eyes!
It was real...

SATURDAY

9.00am Atlantis was wonderful, just like home but with a few small differences. As well as mermaids, there were mermen everywhere. Don't often see mermen on TV. Everyone wanted me to stay. **If only!**

12.58pm Bought a souvenir t-shirt and mug and sent a postcard to my cousin Bob.

7.30 Had dinner with Neptune. I forgot my fork but he had a spare. He was a nice chap but needed a hair cut. I had a great time. I couldn't stay, could I?

SUNDAY

9.00am Felt very glum. Time to leave.

9.01 King Neptune arrived. "Stay!" he said. I couldn't.

9.02 The Merpeople swam to me. "You don't have to go" they said. But I did. How could I earn a living in Atlantis? The next day was Monday and **surely** I had to go back to work.

well, **Didn't I?**

MONDAY...

How many different types of fish did you count?